Far-Fetched Pets

YOUR PET PENGUIN

By Bobbie Hamsa

Illustrations by Tom Dunnington

Consultant:
Caryn Schrenzel
Bird Department
Lincoln Park Zoo, Chicago

CHILDRENS PRESS®
CHICAGO

To Dick and Muggs

CAUTION
Far-fetched pets can live only in your imagination. So don't ask for one for your birthday or Christmas. Go to the zoo or visit the library. There you can learn more about your favorite far-fetched pet.

Library of Congress Cataloging in Publication Data

Hamsa, Bobbi.
Your pet penguin.

(Far-fetched pets)
SUMMARY: Discusses the pleasures of having a penguin as a pet, including his ability to punch out paper dolls and fetch the mail on a cold day. Gives instructions for his general care.
[1. Penguins—Anecdotes, facetiae, satire, etc.]
I. Dunnington, Tom. II. Title. III. Series.
PZ7.H1887Yop [E] 80-15588
ISBN 0-516-04484-2

1994 edition published by Childrens Press®, Inc.

Printed in the United States of America.
1 2 3 4 5 6 7 8 9 10 R 03 02 01 00 99 98 97 96 95 94

This is a penguin.
An Adélie Penguin.
Pretend that he is your pet.

He has a white feathered front.

A black feathered back.

Pink webbed feet.

A strong pair of flippers that used to be wings.

And stumpy little legs that make him waddle.

What will you name your new pet?

CARE AND FEEDING OF YOUR PET

It costs a lot to feed a penguin.

He eats only the finest seafood.

And krill, squid, and plankton are not that easy to find.

He will eat crab, lobster, or fish.

And he'll clean his plate of almost anything.

Give your penguin ice water to drink. (But in a very small bowl or he'll swim in it.)

You'll never have to groom your pet.
He takes good care of himself.
All he needs is a nice cold shower.
A blow dryer to fluff his feathers.
Gargle for his fishy breath.
And a little sandpaper to sharpen his beak.

In the spring, you'll notice your pet acts strangely.

He's crabby.

He won't eat.

And his feathers fall out on the floor.

Don't bother taking him to the vet.

He's just growing a brand new coat.

A penguin is a bird all right.
But not an ordinary bird.
He can't fly
(except through water).
He can't live in a bird cage.
Or eat birdseed.
He can't deliver babies to people's houses.
Or messages tied to his legs.
He can't sing.
Or learn to talk.

But he can hatch a few eggs for science class.

MILK
HALF & HALF
BUTTER

Penguins need a cold place to sleep.
Perhaps your Dad owns an ice factory?
Or a skating rink?
Or maybe you live near the South Pole?
If not, buy a great big ice bucket
and keep it full.
Where will you put your pet penguin?

If he's young, your pet is called a chick.

He's gray and fuzzy.

When just hatched he'll fit inside a teacup.

Even when he's all grown up, he'll be littler than you are now.

Penguins are gregarious.

(That means they're always ready for a party.

They're even dressed for one.)

They come from great big rowdy families.

So they're used to lots of noise.
Take him with you to the day-care center.
To recess.
To birthday parties.
And hockey games.
He'll feel right at home.

Your penguin can surf without a surfboard.
Skin-dive without a mask.
Paddle a boat without an oar.
And play baseball without a bat.
(But he's nearsighted,
So don't expect a lot of homers.)

Your penguin loves to dance.
He likes to travel.
He's sweet, loving, and playful.
He's also nosy and curious.
So if you have a secret hiding place,
don't tell *him* where it is.

TRAINING

Your penguin can learn many things.

And once one penguin learns something, all the other penguins will do what he does too!

His beak is sharp and pointy.
So teach him to punch out stickers
and paper dolls . . .
make holes in the wall for your posters . . .
plant seeds in the garden . . .
hook a rug for Mom . . .
or whittle a present for Father's Day.

He can reach nickels lost in storm sewers . . .
open sunflower seeds or peanut shells . . .
find fishing worms in your lawn.

He can eat a cookie and leave the frosting . . .
peck the mushrooms out of your salad . . .
pick the sesame seeds off your bun . . .
and the walnuts out of your brownies.

His flippers can flatten pizza dough . . .
make nice thin sugar cookies . . .
tenderize tough meat . . .
and flip flapjacks without hitting
the ceiling.

He can brush the lint off Dad's blue suit . . .
stir up the bubbles in your bubble bath . . .
and keep rain off the windshield when
the wipers don't work.

He'll dry Mom's nail polish . . .
give Dad a nifty back rub . . .
flag down a taxi whenever you want one . . .
and clap his flippers for your Knock-Knock jokes
(no matter how bad they are)!

You'll be glad you chose a penguin when he's fetching the mail on cold, cold days . . .

bringing you home when you've gotten lost . . .

letting you ride him down a snowy hill . . .

and giving the whole family swimming lessons.

But the nicest thing about owning a penguin is
he will make you laugh no matter what he's doing!

These are only a few of the things your pet can do.
Can you think of more?

If you take good care of him,
your penguin will live maybe 10 years.
And you'll say he's the best pet you ever had.

Facts about your pet Adélie Penguin (Pygosclis adeliae)

Size at hatching: about 40 grams (1.41 oz)

Size of egg: about 2 inches (5.08 cm)

Days of incubation: 33-38 days

Number of newborn: 1-2

Average size when grown: about 14 lbs. (6.35 kg) and 18 inches (46 cm) high

Type of food eaten: Krill (a type of shrimplike animal
in the order *Euphausiacea),* some small fish

Amount of food eaten daily in captivity: 30-50 small smelt (fish)

Expected lifespan: over 10 years

Names—male: none
female: none
young: chick
group: adults live in groups called colonies,
penguins nest in rookeries,
young live in nurseries called crèches.

Where found: Rim of the Antarctic continent and surrounding Islands,
the Antarctic Peninsula, and Southern Antarctic Islands.

About the Author

Bobbie Hamsa was born and raised in Nebraska. She was graduated from the University of Nebraska in Lincoln with a B.A. in English and zoology.

During the course of her life she has pursued many careers including a ten-year stint as copywriter for Bozell, Inc., an advertising and public relations firm in Omaha. For seven years she wrote and produced print, point-of-sale, radio, and television commercials for Mutual of Omaha's Wild Kingdom, the Emmy-award winning wildlife series starring Marlin Perkins and Jim Fowler.

After owning and running a deli in Sonoma, California, she is now back in the Midwest in pursuit of a nursing career. She splits her time between Grand Island, Nebraska, where her parents, Dr. and Mrs. R.A. Hamsa, reside.

Bobbie is divorced and the parent of a son, John, a recent graduate of the California Culinary Academy.

About the Artist

Tom Dunnington has his home and studio in Oak Park, Illinois. He divides his time between illustrating books for children, painting wildlife subjects, working with young people in the community, and being a card-carrying "grampa" for his seven wonderful grandchildren. Tom has done many books for Childrens Press and considers himself a most fortunate man because his work is fun.